A Dog's Day

The first thing Rosie noticed when she woke up was the bright sunshine.

2

"Ahhh," she stretched. "It's a perfect day to take Rusty on a nice, long walk. He'll love it!"

But when Rosie came downstairs, she noticed something terrible. The door was wide open!

4

"Oh, no!" she cried.

"Rusty! RUUUSTY!"

5

Rosie ran outside, hoping
to find him in her garden.
But all she found was a big,
muddy flower bed.

"That naughty dog has done it again!"
she said. "I bet I know where he's gone..." 7

Rosie went to the butcher's shop. The window was covered in paw prints and dog spit! "I'm on the right path," she thought.

8

"Mrs Butcher, have you seen my dog?" Rosie asked.

The butcher pointed down the street towards the shoe shop.

9

"Hello there!" Rosie said to the shoe salesman as she picked up a shoe.

The shoe shop was a mess!

10

"Uh, oh. . ." Rosie said. "You haven't seen my dog, have you?"

The salesman pointed towards the fountain.

Rosie sat by the fountain. "How will I ever find Rusty?" she thought. "That naughty dog is my best friend in the whole world!"

Just then, Rosie noticed some wet paw prints on the ground. She followed them into the park. And there, in the distance, she saw...

"rrrRRUUSTY!"

Rosie yelled
with excitement.

"There you are, Rusty!" Rosie cried, happily. "I've found you at last!"

"There you are, Girl!" Rusty wagged, happily, "I missed you and I missed my breakfast!"

"rrrRRUUSTY!"

Rusty decided to head home through his favourite park.

"Hey... someone's calling my name!" thought Rusty. "It's Girl! What a lovely surprise!"

14

Splatter!

"What a nice break!" Rusty thought,
as he shook himself dry. "Look at
all those people eating lunch.
That reminds me, I'm still hungry!
I need to find Girl!"

13

Splash!

After all his shopping, Rusty needed to cool down.
The fountain looked perfect! "Girl never
lets me go in here!" Rusty woofed.

"Oh no! I think I might
be in trouble again!"
Rusty whimpered.

9

After the butcher's shop, Rusty sneaked into the shoe shop. "Great! At least I've found some shoes to chew instead!" Rusty thought.

But the man working at the shoe shop did not seem very happy to see Rusty.

8

"Shoo, dog!" said the butcher.

"Oh, why won't that grumpy woman give me anything to eat?" Rusty whined loudly. 7

When Rusty reached town, he looked around hungrily. "Oooh, I can smell lots of good things to eat," he thought. But for some reason the butcher didn't seem very pleased to see him!

"No lead for me today!" Rusty thought to himself as he trotted into town. "I wonder where Girl is?"

Rusty stepped outside and rolled in his favourite flower bed. "Ah, this mud will make me smell lovely," he sighed happily.

4

He was just about to wake up
Girl for his breakfast, when he
noticed the back door was open.
"Mmm, what's that I can
smell outside?" he sniffed.

3